CUMBRIA LIBRARIES

3 8003 04745 2479

KV-144-322

Animal Babies

By THOMAS FLINTHAM

■SCHOLASTIC

Out in the field, there are lots of white SHEEP.
With a hop and a skip, the LAMBS learn how to leap.

Swimming in the river is a
GOOSE, loudly squawking.
She's calling to her GOSLINGS
who are chattering and talking.

Down near the burrow
hops a RABBIT in a hurry.
The baby KITS all follow him —
they smile as they scurry!

Up by the stream
   is a gentle mummy DOG.
She watches as her PUPPIES race
   up and down a log.

Down in the noisy yard,
the CHICKENS want to play.
The yellow CHICKS are small and fast,
they run and climb all day.

All along the riverbank,
a daddy DONKEY dances.
His happy FOAL is up ahead,
she leaps around and prances.

Out in the pasture,
the COWS are munching hay.
A spotty CALF is bellowing—
he loves to run and play.

Curled up in the straw,
a CAT is fast asleep.
Her baby KITTEN tiptoes up
and wants to take a peep.

Down in the meadow grass,
a white HORSE is lying.
Her little FOAL is jumping high,
she looks like she is flying.

High on the hill, the GOATS
walk through the flowers.
One KID wants to play a game —
he's been bored for hours...

From far and wide, the babies run...
The friends can't wait to have some fun!